A Beautiful Farewell

A Story of Loss, Love, and Legacy

John H. Callaghan

A Beautiful Farewell

A Story of Loss, Love, and Legacy

For more information:

JohnHCallaghan.com

BeautifulFarewell.org

YourFarewellGuide.com

First Edition

Paperback ISBN: 979-8-9954893-1-3

Ebook ISBN: 979-8-9954893-0-6

Cover design by Julie Felton

Proofread by Maureen Campanile

Printed in the United States of America

For Jess.

Forever loved. Forever missed.

Table of Contents

BEFORE YOU BEGIN

This is Mary's story.

It begins in a hospital parking lot minutes after her mother's death, where she sits in her car feeling completely overwhelmed and afraid that she's about to fail her mother in the last thing she'll ever do for her.

It ends one year later, with herb plants growing by her back door and her mother's essence woven into her daily life in ways she never expected.

Between those two moments, Mary discovers that creating a meaningful farewell isn't about choosing the perfect casket or flower arrangement. It's about capturing her mother's true personality and celebrating who she truly was.

If you're facing loss right now, Mary's story will show you that the overwhelm you're feeling is entirely normal, that you're more capable than you think, and that there's a path forward that doesn't require you to have all the answers figured out on day one.

If you're a funeral professional, you'll witness what today's families need from you, which is often quite different from how the industry has traditionally served families. You'll be introduced to a framework that can transform how you guide families through this experience.

If you're simply curious about how we honor the people who shape us, you'll discover that the way we say goodbye has far more impact on our grief process than most of us realize, and that creating something meaningful doesn't require elaborate planning or significant expense.

If you've already lost someone and carry regret about how they were honored, this story will show you something important: it's never too late. The way we say goodbye matters, and sometimes we need time and perspective before we can craft a farewell someone truly deserves.

Mary didn't know any of this when she sat in that hospital parking lot feeling afraid and uncertain. She just knew she needed help and had no idea where to start.

Her story begins here.

PART I: WHEN LOSS ARRIVES

Chapter 1 - The Hospital Parking Lot

Mary sat in her car in the hospital parking lot, gripping the steering wheel, staring into the distance, trying to make sense of what had just happened.

Her mother was dead.

The words didn't feel real, and nothing around her did either. Twenty minutes ago, she'd been in room 407, holding her mother's hand, watching the monitor and listening to the breathing that had changed over the past hour, growing labored and strange, then shallow, then stopping.

Then the nurse gently said, "She's gone."

Gone. Just like that.

Mary had stayed in the room for a while after her mother passed. She didn't remember exactly how long. There had been things to sign, people to call, and the nurse explaining what would happen next with the body. Mary had nodded her way through all of it without really absorbing the information.

Then she'd walked out of the room, down the hallway, into the elevator, through the lobby, and out to the parking lot, where she now sat with absolutely no idea what to do next.

Her phone buzzed with a text from her brother, Tom, asking how their mother was doing. Mary stared at the message and realized he didn't know yet. She was going to have to tell him, going to have to type out the words "Mom died" and make it real for someone else.

She couldn't do it yet.

Another text came through, this one from her best friend Rachel, saying she was thinking of Mary and asking how she was holding up. Mary's hands shook as she typed back that her mother had died about twenty minutes ago.

The phone rang immediately. It was Rachel.

"Mary. Oh god. I'm so sorry."

Mary couldn't speak. If she tried to say anything, she was going to completely break down.

"Where are you?" Rachel asked.

"Hospital parking lot."

"Are you alone?"

"Yeah. Tom doesn't know yet. Sarah either. I don't know how to tell them."

"Do you want me to come?"

"No. I just don't know what I'm supposed to do now."

There was silence on the other end of the line, and then Rachel said gently, "You need to call a funeral home. That's the first thing."

"I don't even know which one to call."

"My aunt died last year, remember? We used a place called..." Mary could hear Rachel moving around, probably looking something up. "I can't find the name right now. But honestly, the director was too pushy. He kept trying to upsell us on stuff we didn't want or need."

Mary pressed her palm against her forehead. The thought of dealing with someone pushy right now was more than she could handle.

"Wait," Rachel said. "Hold on. One of my clients lost her dad a few months ago, and she kept talking about how amazing her funeral director was. Let me text her and ask who they used."

"Okay."

"Mary, are you going to be alright for a few minutes? Do you need me to come sit with you?"

"I'm okay. Just find out the name."

They hung up, and Mary sat in the parking lot watching people come and go. The world continued as if nothing had happened.

But her mother was dead.

The thought kept circling through her mind. Her mother was dead. The woman who'd raised her, who'd taught her everything important, who'd been there for every significant moment of Mary's life, was just gone.

Her phone buzzed again. It was Rachel with another text: "Hearth & Passage Funeral Home. Ask for David. My client said he completely changed how she thought about funerals. Made the whole thing about honoring her dad, not just checking boxes. She cried telling me about it."

Mary pulled up the number and stared at it.

She needed to tell Tom first, and then Sarah. She opened her texts and typed a message to Tom saying she needed to tell him something. She hesitated, and then she added the painful words—that their mother had died about thirty minutes ago, that she'd been with her, and that it had been peaceful.

She hit send.

The three dots appeared immediately, then stopped, then appeared again. Tom's response came through, saying he was coming to the hospital. Mary told him he didn't have to, that their mother was already gone, but Tom insisted. He said he was fifteen minutes away and told her to stay where she was.

Mary knew she should probably call Sarah too, but she couldn't go through it twice in a row. Once Tom arrived, they could call her together.

She looked at the funeral home number again and wondered if she really had to call them right now, today. Couldn't she just go home, crawl into bed, and pretend this wasn't happening?

But the nurse had said something about the hospital needing to release the body, that there were decisions that couldn't wait.

Mary dialed before she could second-guess herself.

"Hearth & Passage Funeral Home, this is Susan speaking."

"Hi. Um. My mother just died at the hospital, and I'm not sure what I'm supposed to do."

"I'm so sorry for your loss." The woman's voice was warm without being overly sympathetic in that fake way Mary had been dreading. "You did the right thing by calling. We can help you with everything. First, are you still at the hospital?"

"Yes. In the parking lot."

"Okay. That's perfectly fine. Take your time. There's no rush. The hospital will keep your mother safe until we can coordinate everything. Are you the next of kin?"

"Yes. I mean, I'm the oldest. My brother and sister... I just told my brother. He's coming here now."

"Perfect. So, here's what we can do. You don't have to make any decisions immediately. What I'd like to do is schedule a time for you to meet with David, one of our directors. He's wonderful at guiding families through this process. Would tomorrow morning work, or do you need to meet later today if there's some urgency?"

"I don't know. I don't know what's urgent and what isn't."

"Very little is actually urgent, even though it feels like everything is. The main thing is coordinating with the hospital so they can release your mother to us. I can handle that with a phone call. Do we have your permission to bring your mother into our care?"

"Yes, of course."

"Everything else, the service planning and all the decisions that go with it, can wait."

Mary felt something in her chest loosen slightly.

"Tomorrow morning would work. What time?"

"How about ten? That gives you time to process what happened today, talk with your family, and get some sleep."

"Okay. Ten o'clock."

"Can I get your name and phone number? And who will be coming to meet with David?"

Mary gave her the information.

"We're at 428 Maple Street," Susan said. "But I'll text you the address and David's direct number. If anything comes up before tomorrow, if you have questions or just need to talk, you can call anytime. Day or night. Okay?"

"Okay."

"Mary, take care of yourself today. Let people help you. And we'll see you tomorrow."

After they hung up, Mary sat with the phone in her lap and realized she'd done it. First step completed. She'd called a funeral home.

She still had no idea how she was going to plan a funeral that would properly honor her mother. The thought of making all those decisions, of picking the right words and songs and flowers, of standing in front of people and trying not to break down completely, was overwhelming.

Her father had passed away seven years ago, and her mother had made all those decisions alone. Now it was Mary's turn, and it felt like too much. All of it was overwhelming.

Tom's truck pulled into the parking lot. He parked next to her car and climbed out with his face pale and his eyes red.

Mary got out of her car, and they stood there for a moment in silence.

Then Tom asked, "She's really gone?"

"Yeah."

"Was she in pain?"

"No. She just slipped away. It was very quiet."

Tom's face crumpled, and Mary stepped forward to hug him. They stood in the parking lot, holding each other, while their mother's body lay somewhere in the hospital, and the world kept moving around them as if nothing had changed.

"We have to call Sarah," Tom said finally.

"I know."

"And we have to plan a funeral."

"I know."

"I don't know how to do this, Mare."

"Me neither. But I called a funeral home, and we have a meeting tomorrow morning."

Tom pulled back and wiped his eyes. "Which one?"

"Hearth & Passage. They'll bring her from the hospital to the funeral home. Rachel recommended them. She said the guy there is supposed to be really good. Mom said she didn't want a big funeral, but doing nothing doesn't feel right either."

"Okay. Okay." Tom was nodding, trying to pull himself together. "So, we meet with them tomorrow and figure out what to do. We can do this."

Mary wanted to believe him, but standing in the hospital parking lot, the October sun shining as if nothing had changed, with her mother dead and a funeral to plan, she had no idea how to properly pay tribute to a woman who'd lived 81 years of quiet grace. Mary feared she would fail her mother one last time.

Chapter 2 - Walking Into the Unknown

The next morning, Mary sat in the passenger seat of Tom's truck, staring out the window as they drove to the funeral home.

She'd barely slept the night before. Every time she'd closed her eyes, she'd seen her mother's face in that hospital bed, heard the monitor's steady beep, and felt the moment when the hand she was holding went still.

Sarah sat silently in the back seat. They'd called her yesterday from the hospital parking lot and put her on speaker while Tom drove Mary home. Sarah had cried at first, then gotten angry, then cried again. Now she was just quiet, looking out the window with her arms crossed tight.

"What do we even say to this guy?" Sarah asked. "What's he going to ask us?"

"I don't know," Mary said. "Casket stuff? Flowers?"

"Did Mom want to be buried or cremated?"

"I don't know."

"Great. That's great." Sarah's voice had an edge. "We never had the conversation. Now we get to guess."

"Don't," Tom said quietly.

"Don't what?"

"Don't be angry at Mom for dying without leaving us instructions."

"I'm not angry at Mom. I'm angry at us. We should have talked about this. We're all adults. We should have asked her what she wanted."

No one argued with that because Sarah was correct.

Tom pulled into the parking lot, and the building looked more normal than Mary had expected. It wasn't intimidating or overly formal, just a nice brick building with decent landscaping.

"Okay," Mary said, more to herself than to her siblings. "Let's do this."

Inside, a woman at the front desk looked up and smiled at them.

"You must be Mary, Tom, and Sarah. I'm Susan. We spoke on the phone yesterday. David is ready for you. Can I get anyone coffee or water?"

They all said no. Mary's stomach was too tight to handle anything right now.

Susan led them down a hallway to an office with the door already open, and the man who stood up to greet them wasn't what Mary had expected. He wasn't wearing a dark suit. He wore khakis and a button-down shirt with the sleeves rolled up, and he looked to be in his late forties with glasses and kind eyes.

"Mary?" He extended his hand. "I'm sorry we're meeting under these circumstances. I know this is the last place you wanted to be today."

"This is my brother Tom and my sister Sarah."

David shook their hands and gestured to chairs arranged around a small table. It wasn't a traditional desk setup with him on one side and them on the other, just a table where they could all sit together.

David began with a question that surprised them.

“What happened to your mother? Was her death unexpected, or did you anticipate it?”

Mary explained the events as simply as she could. The heart condition that her mother had struggled with for years. The day at the hospital. The quiet shift in her mother’s breathing. The stillness. The nurse's kindness. The feeling of not knowing what to do next. She kept it brief.

David listened without interrupting.

"Thank you," he said. "That helps me understand the situation. Also, just so you know, your mother is here at the funeral home in our care."

Mary's breath caught, realizing her mother was nearby.

David paused before asking the next question.

"Tell me about your mother. Who was she?"

The three siblings looked at each other, uncertain about what he was asking.

Tom spoke first. "What do you mean...who was she?"

"After years of helping families through this process, I find that it helps me to know a little more about the person who has passed away," David replied. "What was she like as a person?

Mary felt tears starting again, and she realized that in the twenty-four hours since her mother died, no one had asked this question. Everyone had asked about the funeral, about what needed to be done, about arrangements, but no one had asked about her mother.

"She was steady," Tom said quietly. "When our dad died seven years ago, everyone thought she'd fall apart. But she didn't. She just kept going, kept showing up for us, for her grandkids, for everyone who needed her."

Mary wiped her eyes. "She noticed things about people. If you were having a bad day, she knew before you said anything. She'd just show up with coffee, or call at exactly the right time, or..." Her voice broke. "She saw people. Really saw them."

"She hated being the center of attention," Sarah added. "Absolutely hated it. If we threw her a birthday party, she'd be uncomfortable the whole time. She liked bringing people together, but she always wanted to be in the background."

Mary noticed that David was taking detailed notes.

"What did she love?" he asked.

"Birds," Mary said. "She kept journals about them. Every bird she saw, she'd write down the date, the species, what it was doing. She had dozens of journals filled with observations."

"She had an herb garden," Sarah said. "Right by her back door. Just a small one with basil, rosemary, thyme, and sage. She tended it every single day."

David looked up from his notes. " What I'm hearing is someone who believed in small acts done with care. Does that feel true to you?"

The three of them went completely still because that was exactly right.

"That's exactly what she believed," Mary said softly. "She used to say that tending small things with love was how to live a good life."

David smiled. "That's beautiful. Would you say that's who she really was? Her essence?"

"Yes, definitely," said Mary, and her siblings both nodded.

He looked at all three of them carefully.

"Here's what most funeral homes will do. They'll show you packages labeled gold, silver, and bronze. They'll walk you through a casket room and talk about gauges of steel. They'll discuss flower arrangements and guest books and prayer cards, and none of that will feel like your mother."

Sarah leaned forward. "So, what do you do differently?"

"I start with essence, with who the person really was. And then every decision we make, every single one, gets filtered through that essence. If it doesn't honor who your mother actually was, we don't do it."

He tapped his notes with his pen.

"Your mother was steady and perceptive. She valued small acts over grand gestures. She loved birds and herbs and preferred the background to the spotlight." He looked up. "That tells me a lot about how we should honor her."

Mary felt something shift. It might have been hope, or maybe just relief that someone finally understood.

"I'm a funeral director, but I'm also trained as a Farewell Guide," David continued. "My job isn't to sell you products. My job is to help you create an experience that honors your mother, the actual person she was, not some generic version that fits a template."

Sarah shifted in her chair. "Mom really didn't want a big funeral. She said that after Dad died."

"What do you think she meant by that?" David asked gently.

Mary thought for a moment. "I think she didn't want to be the center of attention. She hated being fussed over."

"So not big," Tom said slowly. "But that doesn't mean doing nothing, right?"

David nodded. "There's a difference between size and meaning. Have you thought about what you might regret if you chose to do nothing?"

The three siblings looked at each other.

"I think I'd regret it," Mary said quietly. "When Dad died, we did the traditional thing because that's what you do. But now, looking back, I wish we'd done something that actually felt like him."

"Me too," Tom admitted. "We were so busy following the script that we never asked if the script fit who he was."

Sarah wiped her eyes. "I don't want to make that mistake again. I want to do something that honors who Mom actually was."

David leaned forward slightly. "Then let's figure out who she was and design something that respects that. It doesn't have to be big. It doesn't have to be expensive. It just has to be true."

The room was quiet for a moment.

"How does that work?" Tom asked.

“There are three steps. First, we will explore her true essence more deeply and gather stories from the people who knew her. Second, we'll design a beautiful service that truly reflects who she was. It can be as big or small as you like, as traditional or non-traditional as you prefer, and it’s entirely up to you. And third, we’ll conduct the service. I’ll handle all the logistics and coordination so you can focus on grieving and honoring her instead of managing the details. Does that make sense?”

The three siblings all nodded, grateful for an easy plan to follow.

"But first, there is one thing we need to decide today. If not today, then as soon as possible. Would you like your mother buried or cremated? That choice affects many other decisions," David asked.

"We don't know," Mary admitted. "We never talked about it with her."

"That's okay. Most families haven't had that conversation. We make the decision based on what serves you now and what gives you the greatest flexibility to honor her life. There's no wrong answer here."

They talked through both options. Burial would result in a shorter timeline, with services occurring within a week. Cremation would give them breathing room and time to plan something meaningful instead of rushing through it.

"What did you choose for your father?" David asked gently.

"Cremation," Mary said. "His ashes are still at Mom's house, actually. On the mantel."

David nodded thoughtfully. "One thing many families don't consider right away is having a place to visit. A place where you can go to feel close to them."

Mary exchanged glances with her siblings. "We never really thought about what to do with Dad's ashes."

"Does that mean we have to choose burial?" Sarah asked, a note of concern in her voice.

"Not at all," David said. "You can choose cremation and still have a place in a local cemetery. Many families do both. They have their loved one cremated for the flexibility it provides, and then they place the urn in a cemetery plot or columbarium niche. That gives you the time you need to plan something meaningful, and it also gives you a permanent place to visit when you want to feel close to them."

Tom leaned forward. "We could put both of them together?"

"Absolutely. Your mother and father could be placed together in the same plot. You'd have one place for both of them."

Mary hadn't realized how much the idea of her mother's ashes sitting on a shelf somewhere had been bothering her. "Cremation," she said, looking at her siblings for confirmation. They both nodded. “Then we will look into options at the local cemetery.”

"Good," David said. "That's it. That's all you need to decide today."

Sarah blinked. "That's it? That's all?"

"That's it. Everything else, the service, the gathering, how we honor her, we'll design all of that together over the next few days. But you don't have to figure it all out right now."

Tom shifted in his chair. "Can you give us an idea of what this is going to cost?"

"Our cremation fee is $2,900," David said. "Everything else depends on what you decide to do. A gathering, ceremony, catering, those are all separate decisions you'll make together based on what feels right for your mother."

He paused. "The average traditional funeral in this country runs over $8,000. You'll spend less than that because you're making intentional choices about what matters rather than buying a package."

The three siblings exchanged glances. Tom nodded.

For the first time in days, Mary felt like she could actually breathe.

"Mary, let me ask you something. If you could describe in one word the kind of services you'd like to have for your mom, what would that word be?"

Mary shook her head for a moment, then said, "You just said it. Beautiful. I want her to have a beautiful farewell."

David smiled. "Then that's exactly what we'll create together. A beautiful farewell."

"When do we meet again?" she asked.

"The day after tomorrow. That gives you some time to process everything. I want you to start gathering stories about your mother, and I'll send you prompts to help. When we meet next, we'll go deep on her essence and really discover who she was. We'll also work on her obituary together, since that's another way to capture her essence. People will be asking about services, so we'll want to include that information. I'll also send each of you an email invitation to our planning center website. You can go there to provide the information we'll need for the death certificate and obituary."

David continued, "I can meet you here again, or if you'd prefer, I'm happy to come to one of your homes. Sometimes families find it easier to talk in familiar surroundings."

Mary glanced at her siblings. "My place?"

Tom and Sarah nodded.

As they stood to leave, David paused.

"There's one more thing," he said quietly. "Tom and Sarah, you were not with your mom when she passed at the hospital. Is that correct?"

Tom and Sarah both nodded.

"Your mother is here, in our care. Would you like to see her before you go? Some families find it helpful."

The three siblings looked at each other. Mary felt her heart quicken. The last time she saw her mother, she was in a hospital bed with an IV and monitors. What would it be like to see her now?

Tom's jaw tightened. Sarah's eyes welled up.

Each of them thought private thoughts about what it would mean to see their mother one last time.

"Now," Tom said suddenly. "I think we should see her now."

Sarah nodded, wiping her eyes. "Yes. Together."

Mary looked at David. "Can we?"

"Of course," David said.

He led them down a quiet hallway and opened a door to a softly lit room.

Chapter 3 - The Private Goodbye

"Everything is ready," he said quietly. "Take your time. There's no rush. I'll walk you in, say a few words, and then leave you alone. Come get me when you're finished."

The lighting was gentle and cozy, not the harsh fluorescent lights she had feared. Soft instrumental music played quietly. Simple flowers sat on a small table.

In the center of the room, their mother lay on a beautiful sleigh bed, looking peaceful.

Mary paused abruptly. She had been preparing herself for something clinical, but this felt different. Their mother looked as if she were just sleeping.

Mary's breath caught. It was her mother, yet it wasn't. The features matched the face she'd known all her life. But the essence was gone. The life had left her. This was a body that once held her mother, but her mother herself was no longer present.

David spoke softly. "Your mother looks peaceful. This is your private time with her. Touch her if you want to, say whatever you need to say. However you need to grieve. Whatever you need to do, it's okay."

He paused. "I'll be right outside if you need anything. Otherwise, take all the time you need."

He left, closing the door gently behind him.

For a long moment, no one moved.

Then Tom stepped forward slowly, as if approaching something fragile, and stood beside the bed looking down at their mother.

"Hi, Mom," he said, and his voice broke completely.

Sarah joined him. Then Mary. They stood together, the three of them, looking at their mother.

Her hands were folded on her chest. Her makeup was light, so she looked like herself. Her face was peaceful but empty.

Tom reached out tentatively, then pulled his hand back. "I don't know what to do."

"Me neither," Sarah whispered.

Mary took a breath and touched her mother's hand. It was cold. She held it anyway.

"She looks like she's sleeping," Sarah said.

"But she's not," Tom said, his voice thick. "She's really gone."

The three of them stood in silence, each processing the reality in their own way.

Finally, Tom spoke again. "I keep thinking about all the times I complained about her calling too much. I'd see her name on my phone and think, 'Not now, Mom.' And now..." He couldn't finish.

"She knew you loved her," Mary said quietly.

"Did she? I didn't say it enough."

Sarah touched their mother's other hand. "None of us said it enough. But she knew. Somehow they always know."

More silence.

"Remember how she always hummed when she cooked?" Sarah said suddenly. "That same song, over and over. I can't even remember what it was, but I can hear it in my head right now."

"'You Are My Sunshine,'" Mary said. "She hummed it every single time."

Tom nodded. "And she'd do that thing where she'd taste something and make that face if it needed more salt."

They stood there, sharing small memories, touching their mother's hands, crying quietly.

After a while, Mary spoke. "I was so scared to come in here. But I'm glad we did."

"Yeah," Tom said. "Me too."

"I needed to see her," Sarah added. "To know she's really at peace."

Mary looked at her siblings. "We're going to be okay. We're going to get through this."

"Together," Sarah said.

Tom nodded. "Together."

They stood a few minutes longer, then each said their own quiet goodbye.

Mary went to the door and found David in the hallway. "We're ready."

He looked at each of them with compassion. "How are you?"

"Sad," Tom said. "But okay."

"Good. That's good." He walked them toward the entrance. "Take your time over the next couple of days. Gather those stories. Rest if you can. We'll continue this journey together when we meet again."

In the parking lot, they stood by Tom's truck for a moment.

"That was..." Sarah trailed off.

"Hard," Tom finished. "But right."

Mary looked back at the building. "I think we're going to be okay."

"You think so?"

"I think maybe we can actually do this and honor her the right way."

Tom put his arm around her shoulders. "Two days. Then we'll figure it out."

They drove home in silence, but it was a different kind of silence than before. It was less anxious and more ready.

Later that evening, Mary logged into the planning center website and started adding the information the funeral home would need for the death certificate and the obituary. It wasn't much, but it was something, and right now, something was enough.

PART II: FINDING THE ESSENCE

Chapter 4 - Discovering Who She Was

Two days later, Mary, Tom, Sarah, and David were gathered around Mary's kitchen table. David had brought a large pad of paper on an easel and explained that he would use it to guide the brainstorming.

A dozen images were arranged across the table, depicting their mother as a young woman working in her garden, surrounded by grandchildren, and laughing at family gatherings.

"Thank you for collecting these," David said. "Photos help us see the person we're honoring, not just talk about them in the abstract."

He looked at each of them carefully.

"Before we begin," David asked, "would it be okay if I record our conversation? It will help me make sure nothing falls through the cracks, and it will also help me prepare the obituary."

"Of course," Mary said, and David turned on his recording device.

"Today we're going to discover your mother's essence. I'm not asking for her biography or a timeline of her life. I'm asking for the emotional truth of who she was, the qualities that made her uniquely herself. The things that, if we honor them properly, will make everyone who loved her say 'Yes, that was Margaret Tucci.'"

Sarah shifted in her chair. "How do we do that?"

"We're going to have a conversation," David said. "I'll ask questions, and you'll answer as best you can. Sometimes you'll disagree with each other, and that's fine because different people see different facets of the same person. My job is to listen and synthesize what I'm hearing into a clear picture."

He picked up a marker and went to the large pad of paper on the easel.

"Let's start with the question I asked Mary the other day. Who was your mother? What do you want people to remember about her?"

There was silence for a moment.

Then Tom spoke with his voice rough with emotion. "She was steady. No matter what happened, she was steady."

David wrote on the paper in large letters: STEADY

"Tell me more about that," he said.

Tom looked down at his hands. "When Dad died, we all thought she'd fall apart. She'd been married to him for forty years. But she didn't fall apart. She grieved, we saw that, but she also just kept going. Kept showing up and being there for us, for her grandkids, for the people she volunteered with. Like a rock in the middle of a storm."

Mary nodded with her eyes glistening.

Sarah added, "She was the least dramatic person I've ever known. Everything was on an even keel with her. She never made a big deal out of anything. Even when..." Her voice caught. "Even when she got sick, she didn't want us to fuss. She was worried about us, not herself."

Mary added, "When I called her with problems, and I did call her a lot, she never panicked. She never told me what to do. She'd just listen, and then she'd say something simple that somehow made everything feel manageable."

David was writing and nodding. "So steady, calm in crisis, even-keeled. What else?"

"She noticed things," Mary said. "She was incredibly perceptive. She could tell if you were having a bad day before you said anything. She'd just know somehow."

"Give me an example," David said.

Mary thought for a moment. "When my daughter was about eight, she was having trouble at school with some bullying stuff. We didn't tell my mom because we didn't want to worry her. But one day, Mom picked my daughter up from school, and within five minutes, she knew something was wrong. She took her for ice cream, and my daughter told her everything, things she hadn't even told me yet."

"She saw people," Tom said quietly. "She really saw them. Most people look at others but don't really see them. Mom saw."

David added to the list: PERCEPTIVE. ATTENTIVE.

"Did she tell you what to do?" he asked Mary. "When your daughter told her about the bullying?"

"No," Mary said. "She listened and asked questions. She made my daughter feel heard. Then she called me and told me what she'd learned, but she didn't judge me for not knowing. She just helped."

Sarah leaned forward. "That's what she did. She helped quietly and never made a big deal about it. When I had postpartum depression after my second baby, she called me every single day for three months. Every single day. She'd ask how I was sleeping, if I'd eaten, and if I needed her to come over. She brought groceries and held the baby so I could shower. She never once made me feel like I was failing or weak. She just showed up consistently until I was okay again."

Her voice broke. "I never thanked her properly for that."

Tom reached over and squeezed his sister's hand.

David wrote: QUIETLY ATTENTIVE. CONSISTENT PRESENCE.

"Did she need recognition?" he asked. "Did she want people to know about her helping?"

"No," all three of them said simultaneously.

Mary continued, "She hated being thanked publicly. If you tried to make a big deal about something she'd done, she'd change the subject immediately. She didn't help people for recognition; she helped because that's just what you do. That's how she saw the world."

"Tell me about her values," David said. "What mattered to her?"

Tom thought for a moment. "Authenticity. She valued people being genuine over being impressive. She'd rather have a conversation in someone's kitchen than go to a fancy dinner party. She'd rather you show up in jeans and be yourself than dress up and put on airs."

Sarah nodded vigorously. "She couldn't stand phoniness. People who said one thing and did another. People who were all talk and no action. She lived what she believed."

"Which was what?" David asked.

"That small things done with love matter more than grand gestures," Mary said. "She said that all the time. 'Tend small things with love.' That was her philosophy. Her herb garden, her bird journals, her weekly volunteering, her daily calls to us, none of it was flashy or impressive. But all of it was done with attention, care, and love."

David was writing quickly now, capturing phrases as they spoke. He stepped back and looked at what he'd written:

STEADY

PERCEPTIVE / ATTENTIVE

QUIETLY PRESENT

CONSISTENT

SMALL ACTS WITH LOVE

VALUED AUTHENTICITY OVER SHOW

He turned the easel toward them. "Look at this list. What pattern do you see?"

Mary studied the words. "They're all quiet qualities. Nothing loud or flashy."

"She changed lives without making a production of it," Tom added, reading down the list.

Sarah leaned forward. "It's all about small, consistent things. That's what mattered to her. Faithful small acts, not dramatic gestures."

"So if you had to capture her essence in one sentence," David asked, "what would it be?"

Mary thought for a moment, then said slowly: "Mom was steady and perceptive. She showed love through small, consistent acts and valued authenticity over anything showy or traditional."

Tom and Sarah both nodded vigorously.

"That's exactly right," Sarah said.

David picked up the marker and wrote at the top of the page:

MARGARET'S ESSENCE: Steady. Perceptive. Quietly attentive. Showed love through small, consistent acts. Valued authenticity over tradition.

Mary looked at the list. “That feels like her.”

Tom and Sarah nodded, staring at the words.

"Does that feel like a North Star you can turn to when you’re not sure how to proceed?" David said.

Mary spoke first. “Absolutely. That’s her.”

Tom stared at the paper. "You got all that from one conversation?"

"I didn’t get it,” David said. "You already had it. I just helped you organize what you knew."

He sat back down at the table.

"Now, let me show you why this matters so much. Let's say your brother," he nodded at Tom, "wants a traditional funeral with organ music and formal eulogies and everyone dressed in black sitting in rows. And let's say your sister," he nodded at Sarah, "wants a celebration of life with upbeat music and everyone sharing happy memories and wearing bright colors. And you're stuck in the middle trying to figure out which approach is right."

Mary's stomach tightened because this was precisely the kind of conflict she'd been dreading.

"Without essence," David continued, "you argue over preferences. Tom's vision versus Sarah's vision. Someone wins, someone loses, and feelings get hurt. But with essence," he pointed at the paper, "you just ask one simple question: which option truly honors who she really was?"

He looked at them. "So, which is it? A formal traditional funeral, or an upbeat celebration of life?"

Sarah spoke first. "Neither, actually. She'd hate being the center of formal attention, so the traditional funeral feels wrong. But she also wasn't a 'celebration of life' person. That feels too performative, too much like a party she wouldn't want."

Tom nodded slowly. "She'd want something real and authentic. Warm but not fake-cheerful. Something where people could actually connect, not just sit and listen to speakers."

Mary added, "She'd want what she always created for other people, a space where people felt seen and heard. Where real conversation could happen."

David smiled. "Now you're thinking about essence instead of templates. See how this works?"

"Let me tell you about two types of stories, and I want you to help me identify which stories about your mother we need to tell. The first type is Hero stories, stories where she's the protagonist overcoming challenges. These stories show her character. The second type is Guide stories, stories where she helped someone else through their challenges. These stories show her impact."

He looked at Tom. "Tell me a Hero story about your mother. A time she faced something hard and overcame it."

Tom didn't hesitate. "When she came to America, she was twenty-one years old, had fifty dollars, one suitcase, and she couldn't speak English. Her family thought she was crazy because nice Italian girls didn't move to America alone. But she did it anyway. She worked three jobs, lived in a tiny room, and learned English by watching TV and reading children's books. Five years later, she owned her own small business, a tailor shop. That's where she met Dad when he came in as a customer. She built a life from nothing through pure determination and grit."

David was writing. "That's a powerful Hero story. It shows her courage, her independence, and her work ethic. What about a Guide story? Sarah, you mentioned the postpartum depression. Tell me more about that."

Sarah's voice was soft. "I was drowning. I couldn't get out of bed and couldn't bond with my baby. I felt like a complete failure as a mother. I didn't tell anyone how bad it was because I was so ashamed. But Mom knew somehow. She just knew. She called me one morning and said, 'I'm coming over.' She showed up with groceries and held my baby so I could shower. And she kept showing up every day for months. She never judged me and never told me to snap out of it. She just was there, steady and present, until I found my footing again."

Tears ran down Sarah's face. "She saved my life. Literally. I don't think I'd be here if she hadn't done that."

David's voice was gentle. "That's a Guide story. It shows how she helped you through your darkest moment. Both types of stories matter. The Hero story shows who she was, and the Guide story shows how she changed your life."

He looked at all three of them.

"Over the next few days, I want you to gather more stories like these. Text family members and friends. Ask them to share one memory that captures who Mom was. You'll be amazed at what comes back. What we're looking for is a collection of stories that paint a complete portrait, some that show her character, some that show her impact, some that are funny, and some that are tender. All of them are true."

Mary pulled out her phone and made a note. "How many stories should we gather?"

As many as you can provide. We won't use all of them in the farewell itself, but having a rich collection helps us create something authentic. Plus, the stories themselves become treasures for your family to hold onto.

Tom leaned back in his chair, looking at the essence written on the paper. "I never thought about her this way. I mean, I knew who she was, but seeing it written out like that..."

"It makes her visible," David said quietly. "And that's what a meaningful farewell does. It makes the person visible to everyone who loved them. Not a generic version, but the actual specific human being with all their quirks and qualities and ways of moving through the world."

Sarah wiped her eyes. "What happens next? Now that we have this essence, I mean."

"Now we design the experience," David said. "We'll talk about format and what kind of gathering would feel most like your mother. We'll talk about tone, setting, and how stories should be shared. We'll talk about rituals and symbols and ways to create something that helps people participate, not just observe. All of it filtered through essence."

“We can work on the design now, or we can take a break and meet again in a few days. What works for you?”

Mary, feeling mentally exhausted, spoke up first. “Let’s meet again in a few days, that will give us time to collect some stories.”

David stood, approached the easel, took a picture of it for his reference, and then carefully lifted the sheet bearing Margaret's essence. He handed it to Mary.

"This is yours. Put it somewhere you can see it. When you're gathering stories or making decisions or dealing with family disagreements, look at this and let it guide you."

Mary held the paper gently, almost reverently. Words and phrases that somehow captured her mother more fully than a full obituary ever could.

"What about the logistics?" Tom asked. "The practical stuff like death certificates, notifying people, all that?"

"If you go to the planning center website, you'll find a checklist that covers everything," David said. "I'm also going to work on your mother's obituary. I'll start with the obituary information you added to the planning center website and combine it with some of what we've talked about today. When I have a first draft, I'll email it to you for your review. Once it's finalized, we'll post it on our website, and you can share the link on social media."

He looked at each of them in turn.

"Here's what I want you to remember. You're not planning a funeral. You're honoring a human being. Those are different things. A funeral can be a transaction, a checkbox on a list. But honoring a human being is an act of love, and love doesn't follow templates."

Mary felt the tightness in her chest start to release. For the first time since her mother's death, she felt like they were on the right path, not because they had it all figured out, but because they were starting in the right place with who her mother really was.

David said his goodbyes and left them with homework: gather stories, review the essence statement, and consider what would feel true to their mother.

Still sitting around the kitchen table, Tom looked at Mary. "I thought this was going to be awful. Picking out scripture and arguing about hymns and feeling like we were doing it all wrong."

"Me too," Mary said.

"This doesn't feel awful," Sarah said. "This feels meaningful, I don't know how else to describe it."

She glanced at the easel paper David had given her. They had captured her mother's essence.

Steady. Perceptive. Quietly attentive. Showed love through small, consistent acts. Valued authenticity over tradition.

For the first time since the hospital parking lot, Mary experienced something she hadn't dared to feel before: confidence. Not confidence that she knew exactly what to do, but confidence that she was being guided toward something true.

And somehow, that was enough.

Chapter 5 - The Stories Pour In

Mary sat at her kitchen table the next morning with her laptop open and her phone beside her.

She'd drafted a simple text message and sent it to ten people, including family members, her mother's friends, and the people from the literacy center.

"I'm gathering memories of Mom for her service. Would you share one story that captures who she was? It could be funny, meaningful, or just a moment you remember. Thank you."

She'd hit send on all ten messages before she could second-guess herself.

Now, two hours later, her phone was buzzing with responses.

The first response came from her mother's best friend, Elena, telling a story about getting lost in Italy thirty years ago. Margaret had stayed calm and laughed through the whole thing, saying, "We'll figure it out, and if we don't, we'll have a good story." Elena wrote that Mary's mother had made others feel safe even amid chaos, and that she would miss her so much.

Mary read it three times, tears in her eyes, smiling through her emotions. She'd heard this story before, but reading it in Elena's words and seeing how that moment had stayed with her friend for thirty years revealed something about her mother she hadn't fully expressed.

More messages came throughout the morning and afternoon.

Her mother's friend Linda shared how Margaret supported her during a divorce ten years ago by inviting her for coffee twice a week for months until she felt okay again, never making it a big deal and simply showing up consistently.

Tom's oldest son wrote about learning to identify birds with his grandmother when he was eight, and how those walks had sparked his decision to study environmental science. He was still using the old binoculars she'd given him.

One of the literacy center students shared that he was forty-two years old before he learned to read, and how Margaret never made him feel stupid. She celebrated every small achievement and cried when he finally read his first book from cover to cover. No one had ever told him they were proud of him before.

The stories kept coming. Some were funny, like Margaret accidentally FaceTiming her entire contact list while her phone was in her purse, or getting so absorbed watching a cardinal that she soaked her own feet with the watering can she'd forgotten she was holding.

Some were tender, like quietly leaving grocery bags on a struggling friend's porch for months or sitting beside a hospital bed for hours without needing to talk.

Some were just small moments that somehow captured everything about who she was.

By late afternoon, Mary had thirteen stories to work with.

She sat surrounded by tissues, her laptop screen blurred through tears, feeling like she was seeing her mother from thirteen different angles simultaneously.

Her phone rang. It was David.

"How's the story gathering going?" he asked.

Mary laughed, a sound somewhere between joy and grief. "I have thirteen. It’s a little overwhelming, but I love them all."

"That's beautiful. How does it feel reading them?"

"Like I'm discovering her all over again. I knew who she was, but seeing how many people she touched and reading these specific moments..." Mary's voice caught. "I had no idea the impact was this wide."

"The stories do that," David said gently. "They make visible what was often invisible."

"I can't use all of them in the service, can I?"

"Not in the service itself, but you'll want to save all of them. Some might become part of memory cards or a memorial book. Some you'll just treasure privately. And we'll select the key stories to be shared aloud, the ones that taken together paint the fullest picture."

Mary made a note. "When should we meet again?"

"How about tomorrow? Let's meet at the funeral home so I can show you around. Bring your siblings if you can. We'll look at these stories together, select which ones to feature, and then we'll start designing the actual experience. We're ready for that now. Also, the drafts of the obituary are ready, and I'll email them shortly. There are two versions: one very traditional and the other that better reflects her essence. You can choose which one we'll go with."

After they hung up, Mary continued reading the stories and noticed recurring patterns. The same words kept appearing - steady, kind, listener, noticed, present, consistent. The qualities they had described as her mother's core traits were now being validated by dozens of people who had experienced those qualities firsthand.

She pulled out the paper David had given them with her mother's essence written in his neat handwriting.

Steady. Perceptive. Quietly attentive. Showed love through small, consistent acts. Valued authenticity over tradition.

Every story reflected these qualities. The essence wasn't something they had invented or projected onto her memory. It was who her mother truly was, seen by everyone whose lives she had touched.

That night, Mary sat with her daughter in the kitchen reading stories about a woman who'd lived quietly but powerfully, who'd changed lives through attention and consistency and small acts of love repeated faithfully over decades.

Chapter 6 - Choosing the Words

Mary was making dinner when the email from David arrived, the subject line reading: "Margaret's Obituary - Two Options."

She wiped her hands on a dish towel and opened it on her phone.

Mary, Tom, and Sarah,

I've drafted two versions of your mother's obituary for you to review. The first is a traditional format that covers the basics and the timeline. The second attempts to capture her essence as we've been discussing. Both are complete and ready to publish; whichever you choose is entirely up to you and your family.

Please review both versions and let me know which direction feels right. I'm happy to make any edits you'd like.

David

Mary scrolled down to the first version and read through it quickly. It was fine, perfectly acceptable. Born in Italy, immigrated at twenty-one, owned a tailor shop, married Robert, survived by three children and grandchildren. She volunteered at the literacy center, enjoyed bird watching, and gardening. Services at Hearth & Passage Funeral Home.

Nothing was wrong with it, but nothing felt particularly right either. It could have been about anyone. It didn't sound like her mother.

She kept scrolling to the second version.

Margaret Ann Tucci: A Life of Quiet Grace and Steady Love

Mary started reading and had to sit down at the kitchen table.

She came to America at twenty-one with fifty dollars, one suitcase, and barely a word of English. Her family in Italy thought she was crazy. Nice Italian girls didn't move to America alone. But Margaret had a vision for her life and the determination to build it...

Mary read the entire thing twice, tears streaming down her face. This was her mother. Not just the facts of her life, but who she truly was. The woman who believed in caring for small things with love. The woman who noticed when you were struggling. The woman who remained steady while everyone else panicked.

Mary could see that the obituary echoed the words they had used with David. He had taken what they had said and woven it into a narrative that made her mother visible in ways a traditional obituary never could.

Her phone was ringing. It was Tom.

"Did you read them?" he asked without preamble.

"Yes. Just finished the second one."

"Mare, I'm crying in my truck in the grocery store parking lot. That second one, that's Mom. That's actually her."

"I know."

"The first one is fine, it's what you'd expect, but the second one..." His voice broke. "People are going to read that and understand who she really was."

Sarah called two minutes later on a three-way call.

"Please tell me we're using the second one," she said. "Please."

Mary laughed through her tears. "That's what Tom just said."

"The traditional one is so generic," Sarah said. "It could be anyone. But the second one, when it talks about her coming to America with fifty dollars and learning English from children's books, and then connects that to how she helped people at the literacy center..." She paused. "That's the story of who she was. That's the through line of her whole life."

"What about the length?" Tom asked. "The second one is a lot longer. Do newspapers charge by the word?"

"I don't care if it costs more," Sarah said firmly. "This isn't about saving money. This is about getting Mom right."

Mary looked at the second obituary on her phone screen. "There's a line near the end that says her life reminds us that impact isn't measured by volume or visibility. It's measured in patient listening, quiet encouragement, and steady presence." She took a breath. "That's exactly what we've been learning. We honor her by capturing her essence, not by following a template."

"So, we're agreed?" Tom asked. "The essence version?"

"Definitely," Sarah said.

"Yes," Mary said. "Absolutely yes."

They talked for a few more minutes about small edits, whether to include a photo with the obituary, and where it should be published. Then Mary hung up and opened a reply to David's email.

David,

We want to use the second version. All three of us read both options and the essence-based obituary is exactly right. It captures who Mom really was in a way the traditional format just can't.

We don't need any changes. It's perfect as written. Thank you for taking the time to create something so meaningful.

Please go ahead and publish it.

Mary

Chapter 7 - Planning the Experience

The next day, Mary, Tom, and Sarah arrived at David's office. Each carried notebooks full of ideas and the folder of stories they'd collected.

Before they sat down, David said, "I'd like to show you around the building first. We've recently remodeled, and I want you to see the spaces we have available so you can visualize everything as we plan."

He led them down a hallway and opened double doors into a traditional chapel with rows of pews, stained glass windows, and a solemn atmosphere.

"Some families prefer this space," David explained. "Traditional, respectful, what most people expect from a funeral home. We can hold services here if that feels right to you."

David led them further down the hall, opening another set of doors into a completely different space.

"This is our Visitation Suite. This is where you saw your mother the other day."

Mary reflected on that final time together and felt at peace.

Next, David led them to the Gathering Suite, where comfortable seating was arranged in small clusters rather than formal rows. Large windows overlooked an enclosed courtyard with mature trees and a fountain. The lighting was warm and natural. A beautiful painting hung on one wall. A small kitchenette sat in the back corner.

"This is our newer space," David said. "We finished the remodel last year. We wanted to give families more options beyond the traditional chapel. Something cozier and more adaptable. We mainly use this room for Story Circles. It's a time when families share some of the stories you've collected."

Sarah walked to the windows. "This feels different. More like a living room than a chapel."

"That's the idea," David said. "Some families need formal and traditional. Others need something that feels more like a gathering of friends and family in someone's home."

Tom nodded slowly. "This feels better. More like her."

David opened a side door that led outside. "And this is the enclosed courtyard. Private, peaceful, but still outdoors. We can set up tables out here for meals, and there's enough space for people to move around and talk comfortably."

The courtyard was surrounded by brick walls that gave privacy while still letting in light and sky. Mature trees provided shade. A fountain offered a steady, gentle sound. Wooden benches were scattered throughout. Simple. Peaceful. Unpretentious.

"Beyond the courtyard is our garden," David said, leading them through a gate. "There's a gazebo overlooking a small pond. Weather permitting, we can hold ceremonies out here."

Mary looked at the garden and could picture it instantly. People gathered. Conversations unfolding naturally. Her mother's essence present in the simplicity and natural beauty of the space.

"So, you have options," David said as they walked back inside. "We can use any combination that feels right for your mother."

Back in David's office, they sat at the familiar table.

"Not the chapel," Mary said. "That's too formal. She'd hate being the center of that kind of attention. And I don't want people sitting and listening. I want them talking."

"The Gathering Suite," Sarah said. "That feels right."

Tom nodded. "And the garden for the ceremony. She loved being outside."

David pulled out his notepad. "Good. Let's look at the stories."

He read through them carefully, making notes, occasionally smiling or nodding. When he finished, he spread several pages across the table.

"These are remarkable," he said. "You have real depth here. And what's important is that the stories keep confirming the same thing. That's how you know you've identified her essence correctly."

They talked through which stories would be shared aloud and which would be displayed. The flow of the experience took shape naturally. Story Circle. Garden ceremony. A light meal in the courtyard. Three parts, each serving a different purpose.

When Mary suggested the herb plants, something shifted. The idea felt right immediately. Practical. Ongoing. True to who her mother had been.

"Yes," David said. "That works. Beautifully."

They continued refining details. Music. Readings. The dove release. Objects that would quietly carry presence. The bird journals. The cardigan. The reading glasses.

Eventually, the logistics were mostly settled.

They sat back, surrounded by notes and sketches and half-formed plans.

David glanced at the clock, then closed his notebook.

"I'm going to suggest something," he said. "This isn't a planning exercise."

They looked up at him.

"You've done the work. The structure is here. What matters now isn't adding anything else. It's letting this settle."

He stood and gathered his papers.

"I'm going to step out for a few minutes. I'll be in the lobby when you're ready."

He didn't wait for a response. He simply nodded and left the room, closing the door softly behind him.

At first, the silence felt awkward.

Mary shifted in her chair. Tom stared at the table. Sarah folded her hands in her lap.

No one reached for a phone. No one spoke.

The quiet stretched.

And then something changed.

It wasn't dramatic. It wasn't emotional in the way Mary expected. It was steadier than that.

For the first time since the hospital parking lot, the silence didn't feel empty.

Mary realized she wasn't afraid in this moment. Not of doing it wrong. Not of failing her mother. Not of what people would think.

The farewell wasn't a performance waiting to happen.

It was already taking shape.

Tom broke the silence first. "This feels right."

Sarah nodded. "It does."

Mary felt a warmth spread through her body, surprising her with its calm.

"Yes," she said quietly. "It does."

They sat together for another minute, letting the quiet hold.

When they finally stood and walked toward the door, Mary noticed something she hadn't expected.

She wasn't bracing herself anymore.

She was ready.

Chapter 8 - In Good Hands

Mary returned to David's office two days later to finalize details.

She'd been anxious about this meeting, worried that there would be a thousand decisions she hadn't considered, logistics that would overwhelm her, and costs that would shock her.

Instead, David walked her through a single page.

"Here's what's already handled," he said, checking off items as he spoke. "We have taken care of all the necessary paperwork. The death certificate has been signed, and copies have been ordered. The cremation authorization has been completed, and we have the required permits. The obituary has been posted to our website and Facebook page. Oh, and we've notified the Social Security Administration."

Mary nodded, not realizing how much David's team was doing in the background.

"Now for the important part, the Gathering Suite has been reserved for the date and time. Catering has been arranged, with light appetizers and drinks. Herb plants have been sourced, ninety small pots with the same varieties your mother grew. Memorial cards have been designed and are ready for your approval."

He slid a sample card across the table.

The front had a beautiful photo of Mary's mother in her garden, smiling and holding pruning shears. The back had the Mary Oliver poem that her mother had loved.

Mary touched the card gently. "This is perfect."

"I'll have them printed once you approve. Everyone gets one as they leave."

"What about setup for the Story Circle?" Mary asked. "The photos, the bird journals, all of that?"

"I'll handle it. The morning of, my team will transform the space. You'll arrive, and it will be ready. You won't have to think about logistics at all."

Mary had been imagining herself arriving early, frantically arranging photos, worrying if the chairs were in the right position, and stressing over details while trying to grieve.

"You don't have to do that," she said. "We could help."

"You could," David agreed. "But you shouldn't have to. This is what I do. You should arrive as a family member, not as an event coordinator. Your job that day is to honor your mother and support each other, not to manage logistics."

He pulled out another sheet. "Here's what you need to do. Just these things, nothing else."

The list was short.

Tom finalizes his Hero story and rehearses it once or twice to feel confident.

Sarah finalizes her Guide story.

Mary writes her eulogy, five minutes maximum, focusing on essence, not biography.

Mary's niece practices reading the Mary Oliver poem.

Approve the memorial card design.

That was it. Five items. Nothing about coordinating vendors or managing timelines or worrying about whether everything would come together.

"What about music?" Mary asked. "We should have background music as people arrive."

"I'll create a playlist based on what you've told me about your mother. Classical guitar, maybe some instrumental pieces. Soft enough to talk over but present enough to create atmosphere. You can approve it ahead of time if you want, or you can trust me."

"I trust you."

David smiled. "Good. Because the more you can let go of logistics, the more present you can be for the actual experience."

He pulled out one more document. "This is the cost breakdown. Everything is itemized so you know exactly what you're paying for."

Mary braced herself, thinking about the Google searches she'd done at 3 a.m., showing average funeral costs between $7,000 and $12,000, sometimes much more.

She looked at the page.

Cremation and professional services: $2,900, Funeral home facility rental: $900, Catering for 90 people: $1,800, Herb plants (90): $360, Memorial cards printing: $180, Miscellaneous supplies: $320

Total: $6,460

Mary stared at the number. It was significant but not shocking, and more importantly, every dollar was going toward meaning, not markup on caskets they'd never see or flowers that would wilt in days.

"Is this really all of it?" she asked. "There aren't hidden fees or surprise charges?"

"This is all of it. The only thing that might change is the catering number if significantly more or fewer people attend than you estimate, but we built in some buffer."

Tom, who'd joined the meeting, looked over the breakdown carefully. "This is less than I was expecting."

"Because you're not buying a $4,000 casket that gets cremated," David said simply. "You're not buying elaborate floral arrangements that don't mean anything. You're putting money toward what matters: meaning, ritual, bringing people together. The herb plants cost $360, but every person takes one home and tends it. That's $360 for ninety ongoing connections to your mother. That's worth it."

Mary signed the approval form, and the relief was enormous. Not just because the cost was manageable, but because she wasn't being sold things. She was investing in having a beautiful farewell for her mother.

Tom handed David his credit card and asked him to process the charges. The siblings had already discussed how they would split the cost.

"What about day-of logistics?" Tom asked. "Timeline, who needs to be where when?"

David pulled out a simple schedule.

"Arrive at the funeral home by 2 p.m. Guests start arriving at 2:30. They'll have time to browse memory stations, look at photos, read stories, and get settled."

"Story Circle begins at 2:45 p.m. Plan for 45 minutes."

"Farewell ceremony at 3:30 p.m. in the garden. About 30 minutes."

“Light refreshments will be served in the courtyard at 4 p.m. People will probably linger, but the structured portion concludes around 5 p.m. The total duration from arrival to the end of the formal event is two and a half hours.”

He looked up. "That keeps everything moving at a good pace without feeling rushed. People are engaged throughout, and then they can stay and talk as long as they want over appetizers and drinks."

Mary traced the timeline with her finger. It flowed naturally, one thing leading to the next with breathing room built in, but nothing that felt dragged out.

"What if it doesn't go according to schedule?" Sarah asked. "What if the Story Circle runs long?"

"Then we adjust. This is a framework, not a rigid schedule. If people are sharing beautiful stories and the energy is good, we don't cut it off just to stick to a timeline. We adapt. That's my job, to watch the flow and make real-time decisions so the experience feels organic."

He closed his folder.

“Between now and the service, I'll check in with you twice: once to make sure you're comfortable with your parts, and once the day before to answer any last-minute questions. Otherwise, you don't need to worry about any of this. It's taken care of.”

Mary felt tears threatening again. "I don't know how to thank you."

"You don't need to thank me. Honestly, it's a privilege to help families create something beautiful. This, what we're doing here, is why I stay in this profession.”

As they left, Tom said, "I feel like we should be doing more. Like we're leaving too much on him."

"He told us what to do," Sarah said. "Write our stories and let him handle the rest. That's the division of labor."

Mary understood her brother's feelings. After days of intense planning and decision-making, it felt strange to suddenly have so little on her list. But she also recognized what David was giving them: space to grieve without being crushed by logistics.

That night, Mary sat at her laptop and began writing her eulogy.

She'd been dreading this, expecting it to feel impossible. How do you capture 81 years of a life in five minutes?

But then she remembered that she wasn't trying to capture 81 years. She was trying to capture essence.

She pulled out the paper with her mother's essence written on it.

Steady. Perceptive. Quietly attentive. Showed love through small, consistent acts. Valued authenticity over tradition.

She began typing.

PART III: EXPERIENCING A BEAUTIFUL FAREWELL

Chapter 9 - The Waiting Days

The five days between finalizing plans and the actual service felt both never-ending and too brief.

Mary moved through her days in a strange fog. Ordinary tasks felt surreal. She went to the grocery store and stood in the produce section crying because her mother used to call her from this exact store to ask if Mary needed anything. She did laundry and found herself gently folding her mother's cardigan, as if the sweater might disintegrate if handled roughly.

Her brother was managing all the estate paperwork. Death certificates had arrived. Insurance companies were contacted. Bank accounts addressed. Tom handled it all with grim efficiency while Mary could barely remember to eat breakfast.

"How are you doing this?" she asked him one afternoon when he'd stopped by with papers for her to sign.

"By not thinking about it," he said. "If I think about what these papers mean, I can't function. So I just treat it like a project at work. Tasks to complete. Boxes to check."

Mary understood. Everyone processed grief differently. Tom needed tasks. Sarah needed to talk about it constantly.

Mary needed to alternate between total avoidance and diving deep into memory.

People kept calling, relatives asking about the service, and friends offering help. Everyone meant well, but somehow made everything more difficult because every conversation required explaining, updating, and managing others' emotions.

On the second day after their planning meeting, Mary's mother's friend Elena called.

"I've been thinking about the Italy story," she said. "The one I sent you. Would you want me to tell it at the service? Or is it too light? I don't want to be inappropriate."

"Absolutely! I was planning on reading your story, but it would be so much better coming from you," Mary replied.

Mary was relieved to take that off her to-do list.

The next day, Sarah called Mary in tears.

"I can't do this," she said. "I can't stand up in front of everyone and talk about postpartum depression. It's too personal. Too hard. I thought I could, but I can't."

Mary drove to Sarah's house, and they sat in her sister's kitchen drinking tea while Sarah cried.

"Everyone will judge me," Sarah said. "They'll think I was a terrible mother. They'll wonder why I couldn't handle it."

"No one will think that," Mary said softly. "And Mom didn't think that. She saw you struggling and helped. That's the point of the story, not your weakness but her strength."

"But what if I break down? What if I can't get through it?"

"Then you break down. That's okay. This isn't a performance. It's supposed to be real."

Sarah wiped her eyes. "What if I just write it down and you read it for me?"

Mary thought about that. "You could do that, but I think you'll regret it. I think years from now, you'll wish you'd found the courage to tell her story yourself."

They sat quietly.

Finally, Sarah said, "Will you stand with me? While I read it? I think I could do it if you're right there."

"Of course."

The crisis passed. Sarah would tell her story, and Mary would stand beside her offering silent support and ready to step in if needed.

The following day, Tom called.

"I need you to listen to my story," he said. "Tell me if it's okay."

He came over that evening and read it aloud in Mary's living room. His voice was steady and practiced. The story was good, vivid, and clear. It showed their mother's courage and determination.

But something was missing.

"It's good," Mary said carefully. "But it feels a little polished, like you're giving a presentation at work."

Tom looked stung. "What's wrong with being polished?"

"Nothing. It's just that Mom wasn't polished. She was real. Could you tell it more like you're sitting with family instead of presenting to an audience?"

Tom was quiet. Then he read it again, this time looking at Mary instead of at his paper, pausing where the emotion hit him, and letting his voice crack when talking about how hard it must have been for their young mother alone in a new country.

"That," Mary said. "That's it."

Later that afternoon, David called.

"How are you doing?"

Mary laughed, a sound without much humor. "I'm exhausted and sad, and I keep having moments where I forget she's dead and think I need to call her. Then I remember, and it hits me all over again."

“That's all completely normal," David said softly.

"What if no one shares during the Story Circle? What if we invite people to speak and there's just awful silence?"

"That won't happen. It never does. People want to share, they're just waiting for permission and someone to go first."

"What if the ceremony feels weird? The doves or the herbs or something?"

"It won't feel weird because it's authentic. It comes from who your mother was. Trust that."

Mary took a breath. "Okay. Okay."

"One more thing," David said. "Tonight, the night before, is often the hardest night. You can't do anything else to prepare, so your mind spins. Try to be gentle with yourself. Get some sleep if you can. Tomorrow you'll need your energy."

After they hung up, Mary sat on her couch holding her mother's cardigan.

She thought about the parking lot two weeks ago, her paralysis, and her certainty that she would fail.

She thought about everything since then: discovering essence, gathering stories, designing an experience that felt true to who her mother had been.

They'd created something meaningful. She knew that.

That night, Mary couldn't sleep.

She read through some of the stories people had sent and let herself cry fully, alone in the dark, where no one needed her to be strong.

Around 2 a.m., she went to the kitchen and made tea, Chamomile with honey, her mother's favorite kind.

She sat at the table in her mother's cardigan, drinking tea and looking at the herb plant David had sent as a sample, a small basil plant in a clay pot.

Tend small things with love.

That's what her mother had believed. That's how she'd lived.

Tomorrow, they would honor that.

Mary finished her tea, washed the cup, and went back to bed.

Chapter 10 - A Beautiful Farewell

By 2:30 p.m. the next day, the Gathering Suite was filling with people. Mary stood near the entrance, greeting arrivals, hugging her mother's friends, receiving condolences from neighbors, and exchanging quiet words with the literacy center volunteers.

As people entered the room, instead of standing awkwardly and making small talk, they immediately connected with what was there. They gravitated toward the photo displays, pointing at images and sharing memories. They picked up the bird journals and read her mother's careful observations. They browsed the printed stories on the walls, pausing to read, sometimes crying, sometimes smiling.

The room was filled with quiet conversation. Not the stiff, formal atmosphere Mary had feared, but something warm and real. People were already remembering together before anything official had started.

At 2:45 p.m., David moved to the center of the room and spoke clearly and warmly.

"Welcome. Thank you for being here. We're gathered to honor Margaret, support one another, and remember together. This won't be a traditional service with formal speeches; Margaret valued genuine connection over ritual, so we'll share stories."

He explained that some people had prepared specific stories, and then they would invite everyone to share memories. He read the essence statement they'd discovered: "Margaret was steady, perceptive, quietly attentive. She showed love through small, consistent acts. She valued authenticity over tradition."

Then David invited the speakers to share their stories.

Tom stood and told the story about their mother coming to America at twenty-one with fifty dollars and one suitcase, building a life from nothing through sheer determination.

Sarah, with Mary standing beside her for support, shared the story about her postpartum depression and how their mother showed up every single day for three months, never judging, just being present until Sarah found her way back.

Elena shared the story about getting lost on a mountain road in Italy, describing how she panicked while Margaret laughed and said, "We'll figure it out, and if we don't, we'll have a great story." The room relaxed into laughter, recognizing that typical response.

Then David invited others to share. After a moment of silence, the stories began flowing. Martin from the literacy center talked about learning to read at forty-two. Linda, the neighbor, shared how the twice-weekly coffee visits helped her get through her divorce. Tom's son described learning to identify birds and how those walks inspired his decision to study environmental science.

The stories kept coming. Funny stories, serious stories, tiny moments that revealed character. Each one showed Margaret noticing someone, showing up for them, and being steady and present in small, consistent ways.

Mary sat listening, tears streaming down her face, discovering her mother again and again through others' memories. Her mother had lived so quietly, never seeking recognition, but the stories revealed what her humility had hidden: a life of extraordinary influence lived through ordinary moments of care.

At 3:30 p.m., when the energy naturally shifted, David gently transitioned. "These stories are such a gift. Let's carry them with us as we move into the garden for our farewell ceremony. The restrooms are just down the hall if anyone needs them."

Outside, the October afternoon was perfect with a clear sky and mild temperature. David had arranged chairs in a semicircle facing a small memorial table with a framed photo of Margaret in her garden. Also on the table was a white candle, and the ninety herb plants arranged beautifully.

Tom's daughter sang "Be Thou My Vision," the hymn Margaret had loved from her Catholic childhood. Her young voice was thin at first, but strengthened as she sang, and people who knew the hymn hummed along quietly.

Mary stepped forward wearing her mother's gray cardigan and delivered her eulogy, speaking about how her mother believed in caring for small things with love, not with grand gestures, but through daily acts, the small things others often overlooked. She explained that everyone would take home an herb plant to nurture and use, and when they did, they would remember that small acts of love, when done consistently, are how we honor the people who have shaped us.

Sarah's daughter read the Mary Oliver poem "The Summer Day."

Tom lit the memorial candle with shaking hands. "For Mom. Steady light in our lives."

David gestured toward two people standing nearby with a wicker basket. "Our final ritual is the dove release. A dove has been a symbol of peace and the soul's journey for thousands of years. We will release two doves; one for Margaret and one for her late husband, Robert."

The family gathered around the basket. On David's signal, they lifted the lid together. For a moment, nothing happened, then the doves flew up, two beautiful white shapes rising together into the blue October sky as the chorus filled the garden:

Everyone watched with faces turned upward as the doves circled once, twice, then flew away toward the west.

Mary felt something new. Not closure, because grief doesn't close, but transition. Movement from holding on to holding love while letting go.

Tom spoke to the gathering. "Our mom has been honored. Please join us in the courtyard for refreshments."

The courtyard tables were beautifully arranged with light appetizers and drinks. As people ate and talked, the conversation flowed smoothly. Stories stacked on stories, with laughter blending with tears. It was genuine, messy, and human.

Mary looked around at other tables and saw her brother deep in conversation with their mother's book club friends, her sister laughing through tears with cousins, and children eating cookies and sharing memories of Grandma.

This was what her mother had valued. Real people having real conversations, connecting authentically, supporting each other.

Mary's aunt came to sit beside her. "This was beautiful, Mary. I thought you'd do a traditional Mass, but you were right. She would have loved this. You honored your mother well."

Hearing those words, Mary felt a sense of relief. The fear that had driven her since the parking lot, the fear of failing her mother, was finally gone.

As people started leaving around 5 p.m., each stopped to pick out an herb plant. Mary heard someone say, "I'll plant this by my front door, just like Margaret had hers." Someone else said, "I'm going to use these herbs and think of her every time."

Elena was one of the last to leave. "I'm taking basil. Margaret and I used to make pesto together every summer. I'll make it again this year and think of her." She picked up her plant and walked away, cradling that small pot of basil as if it were priceless.

By 5:30 p.m., only the family remained. David found Mary as she walked through the Gathering Suite one last time.

"How do you feel?" he asked.

"Sad. Exhausted. But also relieved. Is that weird?"

Not at all. You've been carrying the burden of planning and fearing you'd let her down. Today, you did what you needed to do. You honored her. Now you can focus on grieving without that weight.

In the parking lot under the early evening sky, the siblings stood together one more time.

"We did it," Tom said.

"She was honored," Mary said. "Really, truly honored."

They hugged, all three of them together, then parted ways for their cars.

Mary drove home with her husband behind the wheel, her children sleeping in the back, and four herb plants on her lap, one of each variety. She planned to plant them by her back door, just like her mother had.

The day had been beautiful, hard but beautiful, sad but meaningful.

The Story Circle made her visible to the community. The farewell ceremony honored her with beauty and meaning. The refreshments continued the connection and helped people linger in her memory.

Mary looked down at the basil plant in her lap, a small, simple thing, but it carried her mother's lesson: tend small things with love.

That's what she would do. Plant these herbs, water them faithfully, use them when she cooked, and remember her mother every time.

The relationship hadn't ended at death. It had transformed.

She thought about her father, and it occurred to her how different this experience was from his funeral. She couldn't help but regret that they hadn't done something like this for him.

That night, exhausted beyond measure, Mary fell asleep wearing her mother's cardigan, and for the first time since the hospital, she slept through the night.

Chapter 11 - The Return

The next morning, Mary woke up early, her body sore from exhaustion but her mind already racing through what needed to be done next.

They were supposed to return to the funeral home at ten to pick up their mother's ashes and gather the photos and materials from yesterday.

She'd been dreading it. The thought of walking back into that building and reducing everything to ashes in a box felt like a regression. Yesterday had been beautiful, but this morning felt like cleanup duty.

At 9:55, Mary pulled into the funeral home parking lot, the same place where two weeks ago she'd sat paralyzed with fear.

Tom arrived a minute later, then Sarah. They stood together near the entrance, none of them quite ready to go in.

"This feels weird," Sarah said. "After yesterday, coming back for what?"

"Should we just get it over with?" Tom asked.

Mary noticed Tom had a slight smile, which seemed strange given the circumstances, but she said nothing.

They walked in together.

David was waiting in the lobby. "Good morning, everything is ready for you."

He led them down a quiet hallway to a private room.

Inside, soft morning light filtered through gauze curtains. On the center table, illuminated by a small overhead light, sat a stunning urn. It was a handmade ceramic piece, glazed in deep blue and green with intricate leaf patterns etched into the surface.

On the wall hung a portrait of their mother sitting in her garden, surrounded by herbs and flowers, with that gentle, perceptive expression they all knew so well.

And on the side table sat a leather-bound book containing the transcribed stories from the service.

Music was playing softly in the background.

Mary looked around the room, taking in the portrait on the wall, the leather-bound book, and the stunning urn. She turned to Tom. "You did this?"

Tom nodded, looking a bit sheepish. "I called David a few days ago. I wanted this morning to be special too, not just administrative. So I commissioned the portrait, the storybook, and selected that urn."

Sarah's eyes widened. "Tom, this must have cost..."

"My treat," Tom interrupted gently. "I wanted to do one more thing for Mom."

David spoke quietly from the doorway. "Tom had a clear vision. My team just helped execute it."

Sarah's hand shot up to her mouth. "Seeing it all together like this..."

Mary walked to the urn and gently touched it. "The colors are perfect. Just like her garden."

David stood quietly by the door. "Take your time. The room is yours. The portrait and storybook will be wrapped and ready when you leave."

He left them alone.

Tom picked up the book and opened it reverently. Inside, beautifully typeset, were all the stories. Elena's Italy adventure, the literacy student's testimony, and his nephew's bird-watching memory.

The three siblings stood together in the carefully crafted space, their mother's portrait watching over them while her ashes rested in a beautiful urn.

They stayed for nearly an hour. They didn't need to, but the space invited them to linger, to transition, and to say one more private goodbye.

Before they left, Mary hugged David with a real hug, not just a professional thank-you.

"Thank you for seeing her," Mary said, "and for guiding us."

"It was my honor," David replied. "Truly."

They said their goodbyes and drove home, each carrying pieces of their mother's life that had been carefully preserved and beautifully honored.

That evening, Mary set the urn on her mantel where the afternoon light would illuminate it. Sarah hung the portrait in her dining room, where her mother had sat for many family meals. Tom placed the storybook on his coffee table within easy reach.

The beautiful farewell hadn't ended yesterday. It would continue in daily rituals, in stories retold, in herbs grown and recipes shared, and lessons passed down.

Mary stood at her back door, feeling the weight of her mother's cardigan on her shoulders. She'd said she wanted a beautiful farewell, and it had been, including this morning's unexpected gift from her brother.

PART IV: CARRYING THEM FORWARD

Chapter 12 - The First Months

Mary woke the next morning with nothing to do.

For two weeks, she had been constantly moving, planning, coordinating, making decisions, and working through the checklist David provided. Each day had clear structure and purpose.

Now there was silence.

She lay in bed until eleven, which she never did. Her husband had taken the kids somewhere to give her space, and the house was empty.

She finally got up, made coffee, and sat at the kitchen table still wearing her mother's cardigan. The herb plants sat on the counter where she'd left them the night before. She should plant them, but the thought of doing anything felt overwhelming.

Her phone buzzed with text messages from her brother, her sister, and Elena. Mary responded briefly, then turned her phone face down and stared at her coffee.

The grief that had been pushed aside by planning and logistics flooded in like a wave. Her mother was dead, really, truly, and forever gone. The service was over, and the public tribute was done. Now came the part no one prepared her for: living without Mom.

She cried at the kitchen table for an hour, not the gasping, shocking grief of those first days but something deeper and heavier.

Mary sat at the kitchen table for another hour before she finally picked up her phone and scrolled through her contacts. She stopped at David's number.

He'd said to call if she needed anything. Did this count? Was it appropriate to call your funeral director because you were falling apart?

She pressed dial before she could second-guess herself.

"Mary?" David answered on the second ring. "How are you doing?"

"Not good," she said, her voice rough from crying. "I thought I'd feel better after the service, but I feel worse. Is that normal?"

"Completely normal. You've been running on adrenaline for two weeks, and now it's worn off. Can we talk? I can come by if that would help, or we can just talk now."

"Could you come by? I know that's probably weird."

"It's not weird at all. Give me twenty minutes."

When he arrived with coffee, Mary felt a wave of relief. Someone understood. Someone who'd seen this before.

They sat at her kitchen table, and David said gently, "Talk to me. What's happening?"

"Everything hurts," Mary said. "And everyone else seems to be moving on, but I can't. I thought I'd feel better after the service."

“It doesn't make it hurt any less. It just gives the hurt some meaning. There's a difference.”

He pulled out a folder from his bag. "Here are some resources, including grief counselors, support groups, and books that might help. You don't have to use any of it, but it's here if you need it."

They talked for quite a while. Mary did most of the talking, and David mostly listened. Eventually, he got up to leave. "Plant those herbs today if you can, even if it's the only thing you do. One small act, tangible, connected to your mother. It'll help."

After he left, Mary sat for a long time. Then she got the pots, found a trowel and potting soil in the garage, and went to her back door. She planted them in the same configuration her mother had used, with basil closest to the door, rosemary on the left, and thyme and sage on the right.

It took thirty minutes, and by the end her hands were dirty and she was crying again, but the plants were in the ground. Small things tended with love.

The first month was brutal. Physical grief surprised her; the body aches, brain fog, and exhaustion that sleep couldn't fix, while everyone else seemed to move on with their lives.

She returned to work after three weeks, and it was horrible. She couldn't concentrate and cried in the bathroom twice. Her boss recommended she take more time off, but staying home felt even worse because, at least at work, she had some structure.

At night, she'd reach for her phone to call her mother before recalling she couldn't. That moment of forgetting and then remembering was like being stabbed fresh each time.

Six weeks after the service, Mary started sorting through her mother's house with Sarah. They'd agreed to do it together, taking it slowly, one room at a time.

Every object was a memory. The reading glasses on the side table, the bookmark still in the novel their mother had been reading.

They found the box of recipe cards in the kitchen, with hundreds of them spanning decades, all stained, worn, and covered in their mother's notes.

"I want to cook all of these," Mary said. "Every single recipe."

"That'll take years."

"Good. Then she's with me for years."

The holidays were hard. Thanksgiving came, then Christmas, but Mary tried to honor her mother through the rituals they'd built together.

Four months after the service, while cleaning out the garage, Mary discovered a box of her mother's recipe cards tucked behind paint cans. Comfort food recipes with notes in the margins: "Tom's favorite," "Best made on rainy days."

Mary sat on the concrete floor and cried. Not the sharp grief of those first days, but something softer. Her mother was still here, present in these stained cards, in the meals Mary would cook, and in the relationship that hadn't ended but had simply changed form.

Mary stood, carefully holding the box of recipe cards, and carried it into the house.

Chapter 13 - It's Never Too Late

Two months after their mother's funeral, the three siblings sat in Tom's kitchen drinking coffee on a Saturday morning. The kids played in the backyard, and the house was filled with the warm chaos of extended family.

Sarah was the one who brought it up.

“I've been thinking about Dad a lot lately, especially about his funeral.”

Tom and Mary both went quiet.

"It wasn't right," Sarah continued. "We went with Mom to a funeral home, picked out a casket, had that generic service with the organ music and the pastor who didn't really know him. Then he was cremated, and we never did anything else."

"It's what people do," Tom said, but his voice lacked conviction.

"It's what we thought we were supposed to do," Mary corrected. "But after what we created for Mom..." She trailed off, unable to finish the thought.

"Dad deserved better," Sarah said flatly. "He was in the Navy for ten years. He ran that hardware store for thirty. He taught all three of us how to fix things, to be patient, and to solve problems. And we gave him a cookie-cutter funeral that could have been for anyone."

Tom set down his coffee cup. "Every time I think about Mom's service and how we captured who she really was, I think about Dad's funeral and feel like we failed him."

"Let's do something about it," Mary said.

Both siblings looked at her.

"It's been seven years," Tom said. "Isn't it too late?"

Mary grabbed her phone and said, "Let me call David."

Twenty minutes later, David called back.

"It's absolutely not too late," he said when Mary explained what they wanted to do. "I work with families on retrospective tributes regularly. Can you come in tomorrow?"

The next afternoon, they sat in David's familiar office.

"What you're planning is exactly right," David said. "Your father deserves to be honored properly, and the fact that seven years have passed doesn't change that."

He pulled a single page from his files and handed it to Mary.

"This is A Beautiful Farewell Framework. It's the roadmap for everything we did for your mother. The essence questions, the story gathering process, the timing - it's all here. You can work through this on your own."

Mary looked at the page in awe. It summarized, on one page, everything they had gone through for their mom. She handed it to Tom.

"This is what you were doing with us," Tom said. "You just didn't show us the steps."

David smiled. "Exactly, I didn't want to overwhelm you. But now you can use it yourselves for your dad. Here's how we can work together: I can handle everything like I did for your mother. Or you can do everything yourself using this framework. Or, you can lead the process while I provide guidance, and my team manages certain production elements."

"Like what elements?" Sarah asked.

"We can create an enhanced obituary, a video tribute, and coordinate with specialty vendors like the dove release company. These are all services that benefit from professional production but don't require me to manage the entire event."

"That's what we want," Mary said, looking at her siblings. "We want to do this ourselves, but we want your help."

"Perfect," David said. "Work through the essence discovery and story gathering. When you're ready, send me what you've found. I'll review it, ask clarifying questions, and help you see patterns you might have missed. Then my team can create the elements you want while you focus on the actual gathering."

Over the next few weeks, they worked through the framework together, sitting around Tom's dining room table.

Who was Robert Tucci, really?

The answers came more easily than they expected because they were now asking the right questions, the ones David had taught them. Their father had been quiet but very capable. He could fix anything. He had served on a destroyer in the Mediterranean. He ran the hardware store not because it was profitable but because he enjoyed helping people solve problems.

"Steady," Tom said. "That's the word that keeps coming up."

"And practical," Sarah added. "Everything he did had a purpose."

"But kind," Mary insisted. "Remember how he'd spend an hour helping Mrs. Peterson figure out which light bulbs she needed, even though she was only spending three dollars?"

Tom nodded slowly. "He did that with everything. When I broke my bike chain, he spent a whole Saturday afternoon teaching me how to fix it myself."

Sarah set down her pen. "He tended things. Not like Mom with her garden and recipes. But he tended broken drawer pulls and loose hinges and confused customers."

Mary felt something click. "Mom tended her herbs and her recipes and her relationships. Dad tended to mechanical things and people's problems."

"They both tended small things," Tom finished. "Just different kinds of small things."

The three siblings sat in silence, realizing what they'd discovered.

They reached out to his old Navy buddies. Tom found phone numbers for three men who had served with their father on the USS Joseph Strauss. Each had stories the siblings had never heard about their father's steady hands during rough seas, his patience in teaching younger sailors, and the way he'd spend extra time making sure every tool was stored correctly.

"Bob tended that engine room like it was his own heartbeat," one buddy said. "Never rushed, never careless. Every small thing mattered to him."

Sarah reached out to former employees from the hardware store. They discovered that their father had quietly paid for one employee's daughter's medical bills, kept a man on staff for two years despite his tremors, and taught dozens of teenagers their first real job skills.

“Mr. Tucci would spend twenty minutes helping a customer find the perfect screw for their project,” one employee told her. “He didn’t care about making a sale. He cared about helping them do it right.”

Mary compiled everything and emailed it to David.

Two days later, he called.

"I've read everything you sent. You've captured him beautifully. The 'tending small things' parallel to your mother is profound. That shared epitaph is going to be incredibly meaningful."

He asked a few questions that helped them see connections they had missed, pointed out patterns in the stories, and validated their work.

"Now, would you like my team to create some elements for you? I can take the original obituary from seven years ago and enhance it with this essence material, the way we did for your mother. Let's produce a video tribute for your dad. Sound good?"

They said yes to all of it.

"Let me review everything with my team, and I'll send you a quote for the production work," David said. "Much simpler than last time since you're handling the venue and coordination yourselves."

A week later, the deliverables arrived by email.

The enhanced obituary took the basic facts from the original - born in 1940, Navy veteran, hardware store owner, survived by wife and three children - and infused them with the essence they had discovered. It told the story of a man who believed in doing things right, who taught through patient example, and who paid close attention to the details others overlooked.

Tom read it twice. "This is Dad. The first obituary was just facts. This one is actually him."

The video tribute was five minutes of photos set to instrumental music, with key stories appearing as text overlays. Simple, professional, moving.

"David's team created all this from what we sent them," Tom said, shaking his head.

Six weeks after deciding to hold a ceremony for their dad, they were ready to go. They gathered at the VFW hall, nothing fancy, just the three siblings and their families, Dad's Navy buddies, the hardware store crew, and a few neighbors who remembered him.

Tom stood and explained why they'd waited seven years to do this properly.

“When Dad died, we did what we thought was expected. We held a traditional funeral. But it didn't truly reflect who he was. Then, when our mother passed away last year, we realized there was another way. We learned that Mom's entire life was about caring for small things with love. Her herb garden, her recipes, the way she made everyone feel seen.”

He paused. "And when we started gathering stories about Dad, we realized he did the same thing, just differently. Mom tended living things. Dad cared for broken things and people who needed patient help. They both believed that small things mattered."

He gestured to the headstone marker they'd brought, the one that would go on their parents' shared grave: They Tended Small Things With Love.

"This isn't just Mom's epitaph. It's both of theirs. And we're doing this gathering today to honor Dad the same way we honored Mom."

One by one, people stood and shared stories. The Navy buddies talked about his reliability and how he'd make sure younger sailors understood not just what to do but why. The hardware store employees talked about his patience with every customer, regardless of what they spent. The neighbors talked about his quiet helpfulness.

When the stories ended, they played the video tribute. Everyone smiled as they watched his life story unfold.

Then they stood together and once again released two white doves, one for each parent, watching them circle and fly west toward the setting sun.

As they cleaned up that evening, Sarah turned to her siblings. "I feel better. Like we finished something that was left undone."

"Me too," Tom agreed. "I didn't realize how much that guilt was weighing on me until it lifted."

Mary reflected on the two services, her mother's elaborate farewell and her father's simpler tribute. Both meaningful, both true to who the person had been.

"You know what this taught me?" she said. "It's never too late to honor someone you love. Even years later, even after you think the moment has passed, you can still create something meaningful."

Tom picked up the A Beautiful Farewell Framework from the table where Mary had left it. "Having this made it possible. We knew what questions to ask, what to look for. David guided us, but we did the work."

Mary took the page from Tom and tucked it into her bag. "I'm going to keep this. The next time someone I know faces loss, I'm giving them this and David's number. Because doing something matters, even if it's years later."

They locked up the VFW hall and walked to their cars. The evening was cool and clear, and Mary felt a sense of completion she hadn't expected.

Chapter 14 - One Year Forward

The one-year anniversary of her mother's passing approached like weather Mary could see looming but couldn't avoid.

She and her siblings had been discussing what to do. Tom suggested they finally bury both their parents' ashes together and mark the year with a simple gathering at the cemetery.

On the morning of the anniversary, Mary woke up early. The date on her calendar was October 15, marking a year since her mother died in that hospital room. Three hundred sixty-five days of living without her.

Mary had survived them, not gracefully and not perfectly, but she'd survived.

She got dressed, put on her mother's cardigan even though the day was warm, and went to her back door.

The herb garden was thriving. The basil was lush and green, the rosemary was woody and fragrant, and the thyme was spreading across the ground. Mary cut a sprig of rosemary for remembrance.

At the cemetery, her siblings were already there with their families. David had arranged everything and stood respectfully nearby, holding both urns. They'd chosen a plot beneath an old oak tree and a double marker to honor both parents.

The ceremony was simple. Just the three siblings, their families, and David, who had come to mark the year with them.

As both urns were placed in the burial vault lining the grave, Tom spoke first. "Together again after seven years apart. That feels right."

The marker they'd chosen read: Margaret Tucci 1943-2024, Robert Tucci 1940-2017, They Tended Small Things With Love.

They had selected the epitaph together after discovering it was true for both parents. It was their parents' essence, distilled into six words.

Tom had brought a small potted herb plant to leave by the grave. Mary brought her rosemary sprig and a weathered photo of their mother in the garden.

They stood in silence for a while. Then Tom said, "It's been a year, Mom. A whole year without you. It's been hard, really hard, but we're okay. We're making it."

His voice was steady and stronger than it had been a year ago.

Sarah added, "We've been cooking your recipes, telling stories about you, and teaching our kids what you taught us. You're still here, just different."

She gently touched the grave marker, running her fingers over both names. "And we finally honored Dad properly, too. We gathered at the VFW and learned so much about him that we never knew. His Navy buddies shared stories that made us cry. The hardware store guys shared things that made us proud. We got it right for him, even though it took us seven years."

Mary nodded. "You would have been proud of us, Mom. We used everything you taught us about tending small things. We realized Dad did the same thing, just with different things. And now you're both here, together, with words that honor both of you."

Mary felt her throat closing as she looked at the grave marker, at the dates that bracketed her parents' lives, and at the words they'd chosen to remember them by.

"We honored you both well," she said quietly. "A year ago, I was worried I'd fail you, Mom, but we did it right. We discovered your essence, told your stories, and created something beautiful. And then we went back and did the same for Dad. We've been carrying you both forward every day since."

She placed the rosemary sprig on the grave. "Rosemary for remembrance. You taught me that."

David stood with them at the grave, quiet and respectful. After a moment, he spoke.

"A year ago, you were afraid of failing her. You didn't. You honored her beautifully, and you've carried her forward." He looked at Mary. "That's what these months have been about: learning to live with absence while maintaining connection."

Tom spoke up. "Going back for Dad changed something for us. We'd been carrying that guilt for seven years."

David nodded. "It's never just about the service itself. It's about discovering who someone really was. You did that for both your parents."

This was family, shaped by loss but held together by love.

Eventually, they began walking back to their cars, and David walked beside Mary.

"How are you really doing?" he asked.

"Better than I was. Not okay, but better. I've learned you don't get over this; you just get used to it."

Mary thought for a moment. "And going back for Dad taught me it's never too late. That's important for other families to know."

David smiled. "The best time to honor someone is when they die. The second-best time is whenever you're ready."

That night, Mary sat at her kitchen table, flipping through an old photo album.

She stood and walked to her back door, where the herb garden was visible in the porch light. She touched her mother's cardigan and whispered into the quiet night, "I miss you both."

The herbs moved slightly in the evening breeze.

IF YOU'RE FACING A LOSS

If you're facing the anticipated loss of someone you love, the weeks and months leading up to death can feel overwhelming. Amid medical decisions, family dynamics, practical concerns, and emotional exhaustion, it's easy to lose sight of what matters most: the person you're about to lose and the time you still have together.

For that reason, a companion resource titled Your Farewell Guide exists. It's designed to help you navigate this difficult transition with intention, focusing on what truly matters while handling the practical realities that can't be ignored.

The guide addresses some of the questions families face during this time: How do we balance hope and reality? What conversations should we have while we still can? How do we create meaningful moments without forcing them? How do we prepare for what's coming without giving up on today?

It's often provided by hospice teams, clergy, and funeral professionals who believe in giving families time, clarity, and compassion during this difficult season.

If you would like a copy, visit YourFarewellGuide.com or ask your hospice team or funeral professional if they have it available.

When the time comes to plan a farewell service, the essence-centered approach you saw in Mary's story can guide you. Start by asking: Who was this person really? What made them themselves? Then let that essence shape everything else.

You don't have to do this alone. Just as a skilled guide helped Mary's family, the right professional can help you discover and honor your loved one's essence. Trust yourself, trust the process, and trust that a beautiful farewell is possible.

ABOUT THE AUTHOR

John H. Callaghan has spent more than two decades transforming the farewell experience by bridging the gap between families and funeral professionals.

After leaving a career in technology in 2003, John discovered his calling to help funeral professionals adapt to the needs of today's families. He's worked with thousands of funeral homes, helping them shift from traditional funeral services to essence-based planning and beautiful farewell experiences.

"A Beautiful Farewell" distills what John has learned from hundreds of real conversations and from personal experience: that the way we say goodbye matters deeply, it's never too late to honor someone properly, and families and funeral professionals need each other in order to create a farewell that honors a life in a meaningful way.

For families facing loss: YourFarewellGuide.com

Join the community: BeautifulFarewell.org

For funeral professionals: FuneralSuccess.com

Personal website: JohnHCallaghan.com

Visit BeautifulFarewell.org to read more stories from families who found their own way to say goodbye.

www.ingramcontent.com/pod-product-compliance
Lightning Source LLC
LaVergne TN
LVHW090527110826
845146LV00003B/1003

* 9 7 9 8 9 9 5 4 8 9 3 1 3 *